Vasuki - The Fursona

Yet again, the stoat-sona has grown. The past few years, I - and Vasuki - have evolved quite a bit. At this point, he's permanently in his winter coat, and he's even more sexually voracious than ever. You'll find no shortage of his escapades within these next few pages.

It seems that with each passing volume, he starts to resemble me more and more. I've tweaked his design to be more in-line with my current age and my "pseudo-dad" appearance, and the results have proven to be very successful with his fans. It's been nice to have a character with which I can express myself sexually so freely.

AH!!!
S-STOP!! LET ME GO!
I'M GONNA KICK YOUR ASS, NERD!
I'D LIKE TO SEE YOU TRY ...
DUMBASS

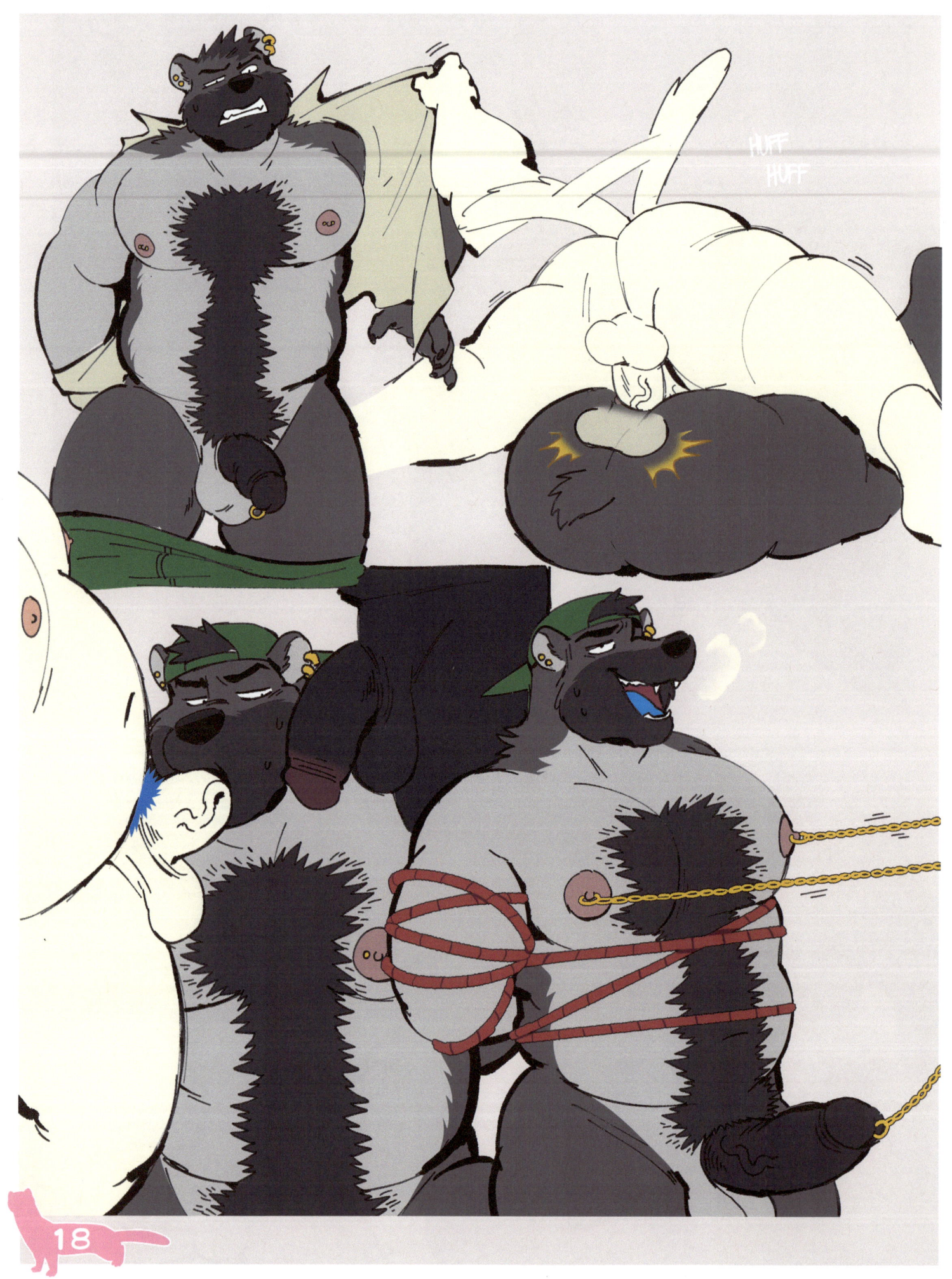

HUFF
HUFF

VASUKI

1999 BIZARRE SUMMER

VASUKI

Mr. Umbra

Since his last sighting, Umbra hasn't been explored much more just yet, but he is still appearing in several sketches, particularly those where Vasuki needs a helping hand.

Mr. Umbra is still a prolific scientist with a lot of lecherous interests and motivations for his pursuits. A wealthy stoat, he has a lot of facilities and devices at his disposal - most of all his visor, which remains a total mystery. Only he knows what it does.

Tre

Tre and his family have become a major staple in my work over the past several years - in no small part due to the very pos-itive response fans tend to have to him. He's a jock, he's a nerd, and he's stacked. That's all you need to know.

He is now pretty synonymous with his family members, including his recently developed "twin" cousin, Trapper, so I'm sort of cramming them both into this section to bring in the wolves.

Trapper

Born very close together, Trapper has always been treated as more of a brother to his cousin, Tre. The two usually get along, but sometimes sparks fly due to Trapper's aggressive nature. He's a good boy, but he tends to get carried away.

Although similar in appearance, to the observant, there are a few differences between the cousins. Trapper has floppy bangs, and foreskin. In terms of personality, he's much more of an assertive, macho jock, though he shares his cousin's intelligence under the surface.

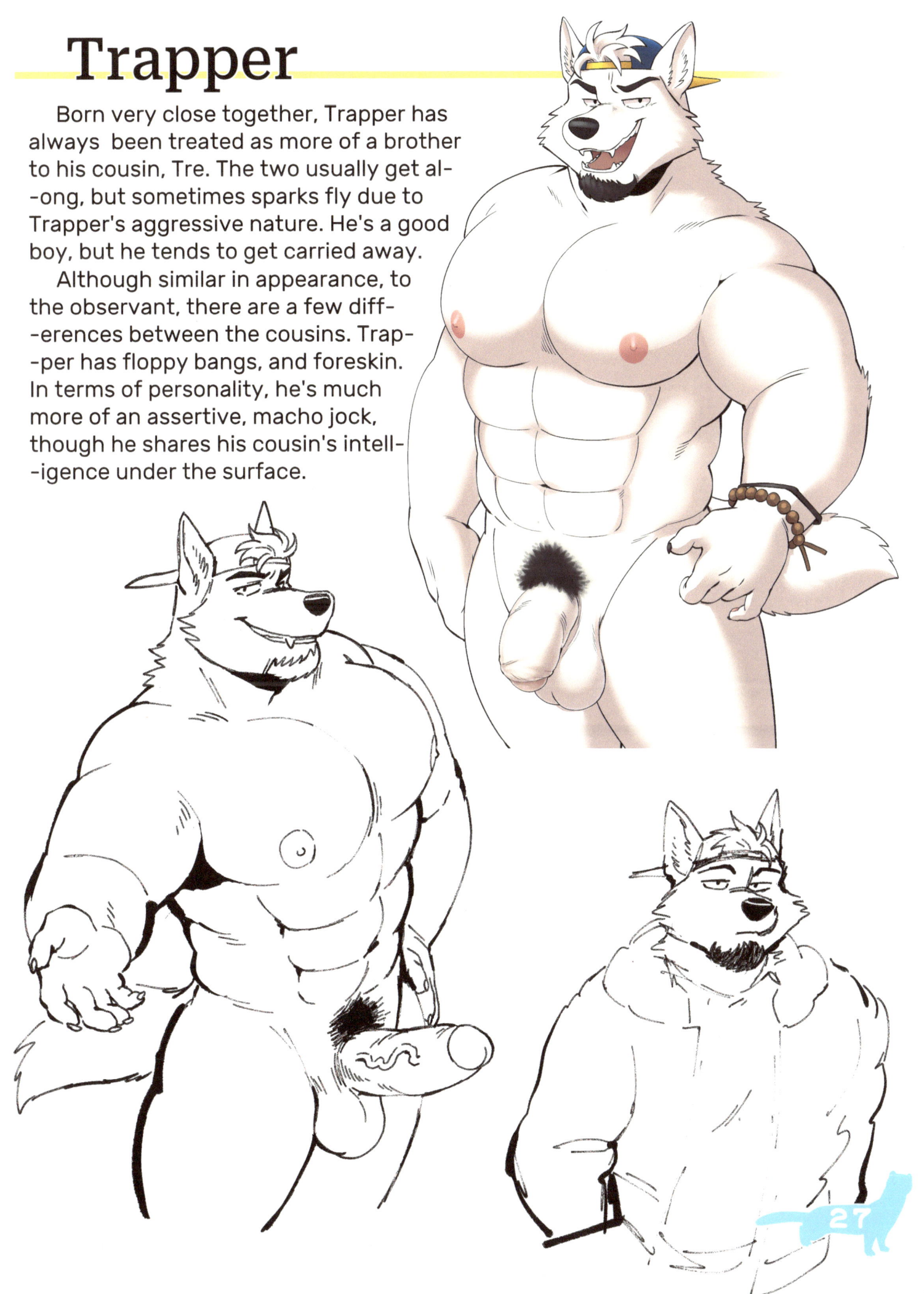

29

31

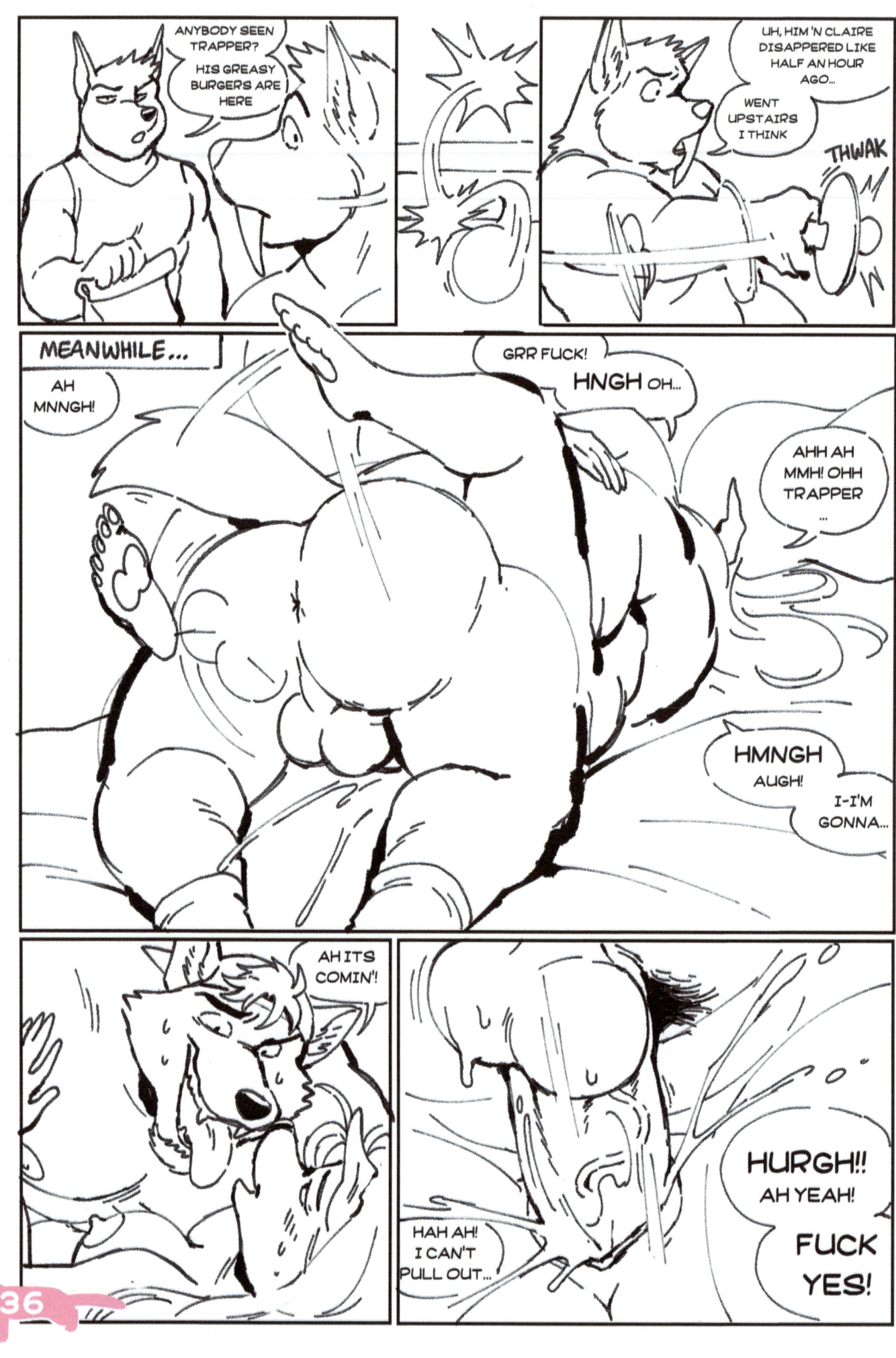

SKIF

WELL, WELL... I DIDN'T KNOW YOU CARED~

DUN GET IT TWISTED, PINKY... ...I CARE ABOUT STEEL

AND FOR SOME REASON HE'S CONCERNED ABOUT YOU...

Future Trapper

Trapper will always be a rowdy college boy, my characters and universe exist in a floating timeline where they really never age beyond their current years, but I do sometimes get curious about the future and like to explore its possibilities. For what--ever reason, I had major inspiration to dip my toes in these waters with Trapper.

Introducing dad Trapper - a late 30s wolf who has chosen to take over his grandpa's company and rules it with an iron fist. This iteration of Trapper is still just as assertive and, frankly, takes no bullshit. Despite this, he is actually a rather lenient boss, following after his grandfather Victor. He seems very scary, and he can be if you really test him, but ultimately he does everything he can to do right by his employees, as long as they do right by him. He has, however, been married three separate times...

41

Kody

Star linebacker, and verified "brick wall" of the Cerberus Watchdogs, Kody is a terrifying bully of a bear that you don't want to go up against. However, you'd be surprised at what is just below the surface - if you can get close enough. Kody neglects his academics, though is fairly intelligent when necessary - similarly, he is an affectionate bear with the right guy. Few earn his respect, among them being his athletic rival, who is none other than Tre.

45

CERBERUS WATCHDOGS
KODY URSAVICH
#56

Brody

Along with a third football team entering the Vasuki--verse, comes a slew of new jocks, one of which is Brody Badger - a defensive linesman for the Tusks. Similarly to Kody, Brody is feared for his resilience and his status as a wall on the field. The son of a wealthy CEO, he tends to be the host of many team parties, as he has a gigantic mansion at his disposal.

Unlike Kody or even Tre, Brody is a hungry power bottom and is either too stupid or just genuinely unashamed to the point that he feels no need to really be discreet about it. Sex in general is a frequent craving for him, and he pursues it without hesitation. As you may have guessed, academics are not on his list of top priorities, but his intuitive intelligence may sur--prise you all the same.

BADGER ATTACK ★ SQUAD ★

CRACK!

Billy

Billy is Brody's greatest friend. The two have been close since early childhood, and even now they are practically glued together at the hips. Both play for the Tusks, and have been on a long journey to "get huge", in the hopes of gaining the attention of their athletic idol, Mr. Gulo.

What started as a deep friendship has been budding into more - to outside observers, Billy and Brody are a little closer than mere friends tend to be. Neither of them have acknowledged the true status of their relationship, but regardless it is fairly obvious that there is a great deal of love and trust between them.

"Twink" Brody

Although huge, Brody was once a more slender boy. I tend to draw him in his enormous, buff form as it is his "current" state of being. When I first created him, however, he was far from being so gigantic, and sometimes I like to revisit this size.

In this state, Brody looks a little more like his brothers, and in general just has a very different vibe that is fun to play with from time to time.

The Brothers

Brody was intended to be a single child at first, but due to a misunderstanding during a stream where someone thought I was drawing three separate badgers, he now has two twin brothers! The idea appealed to me so much that I made it canon. Now that he's larger, he resembles them just a little less, though.

They're all rather different from one another as well. Bryce is a spoiled pretty boy who thinks the girls can't resist him (he's not wrong, really) and Brett is a galaxy brained genius. The three of them are always up to some kind of shenanigans.

BRYCE   BRETT   BRODY

BRODY   BRYCE   BRETT

Buck

This toothy, blue, husky boy is on the rise as a fan-fav-
-orite character, and is one of my personal favorites as
well. Created to be the flagship quarterback for the Tusks,
Buck comes across primarily as a lovable goof, but has also
earned the respect of his peers as an athlete. Like a few
other Vasuki brand jocks, he is not a shining example
of academic excellence - but he does his best and
his heart is always in the right place.

Despite his dental oddity, Buck is actually
considered to be rather effortlessly gorgeous.
Girls adore him, and he is considered to be a
gay boy's dream come true across all three
campuses... regardless of what
his true sexuality may be.

TUSKS
13

Buck's Build

As you've probably already noticed, Buck's build has shifted a little since the very early sketches of him at the beginning of this section. Much like Brody, he went through a bit of a transformaton the more that I drew him. At first he was more of a buff twunk, and by now we're sliding into his current chubby build.

To be honest, I really like both versions of Buck. I think both have something unique to offer, and will probably end up drawing both off and on. Chubby buff Buck, however, is unique for my quarterbacks, which I enjoy.

Buck & Steel

Fellow star quarterback, Steel, is Buck's closest friend and who he turns to any time he's having any sort of problem. The two are basically inseparable, and do most things together. Steel himself is more brain-y than his best buddy, and uses his intellect to get them out of (or into) trouble. The bond between them also strains the definition of "friendship", going somewhat beyond and into boyfriends territory.

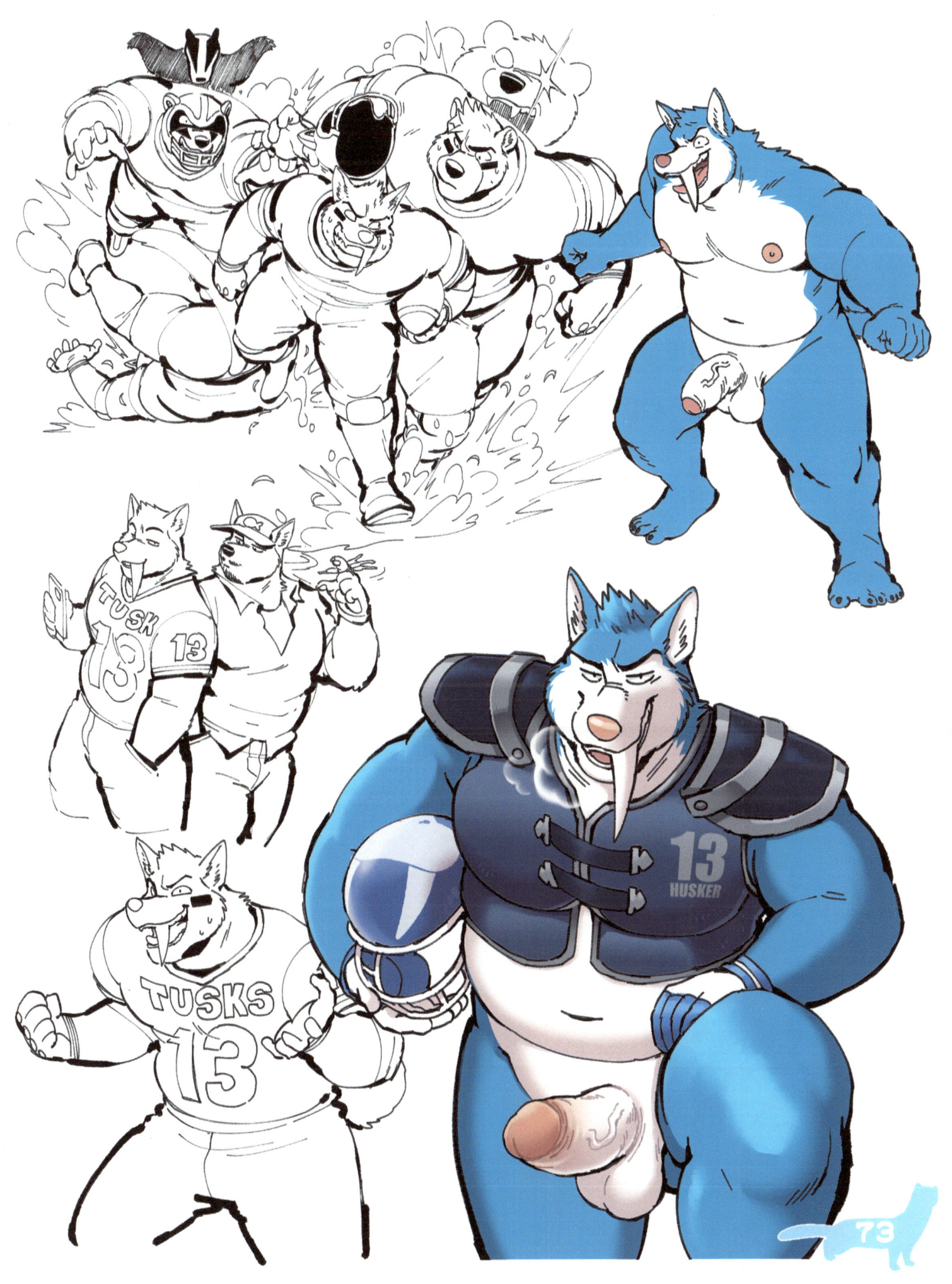

81

Una

The latest and greatest certified gay boy of the Vasukiverse is none other than Una. Following in the footsteps of the likes of Howie - he is a sensual, seductive, and flirty young wolf with a hunger for his fellow classmates - often those of the athletic variety. Unlike his other gay friends, however, Una is also an athlete himself - being a county-wide baseball star for the Tusks. Due to this, he gains the respect of the football teams somewhat more easily.

Una comes from a long line of wolves known as the Lobopez family. Much like the Wolfellers, they have quite the presence in the community. Aside from his athletic skills, he's known for being very playful in general and a reliable shoulder to lean on to his queer friends, being a sort of paternal figure for other gay youths in the area. Despite this, he is not exactly the most responsible boy you'll meet and can even be a bad influence... as long as it leads to something fun.

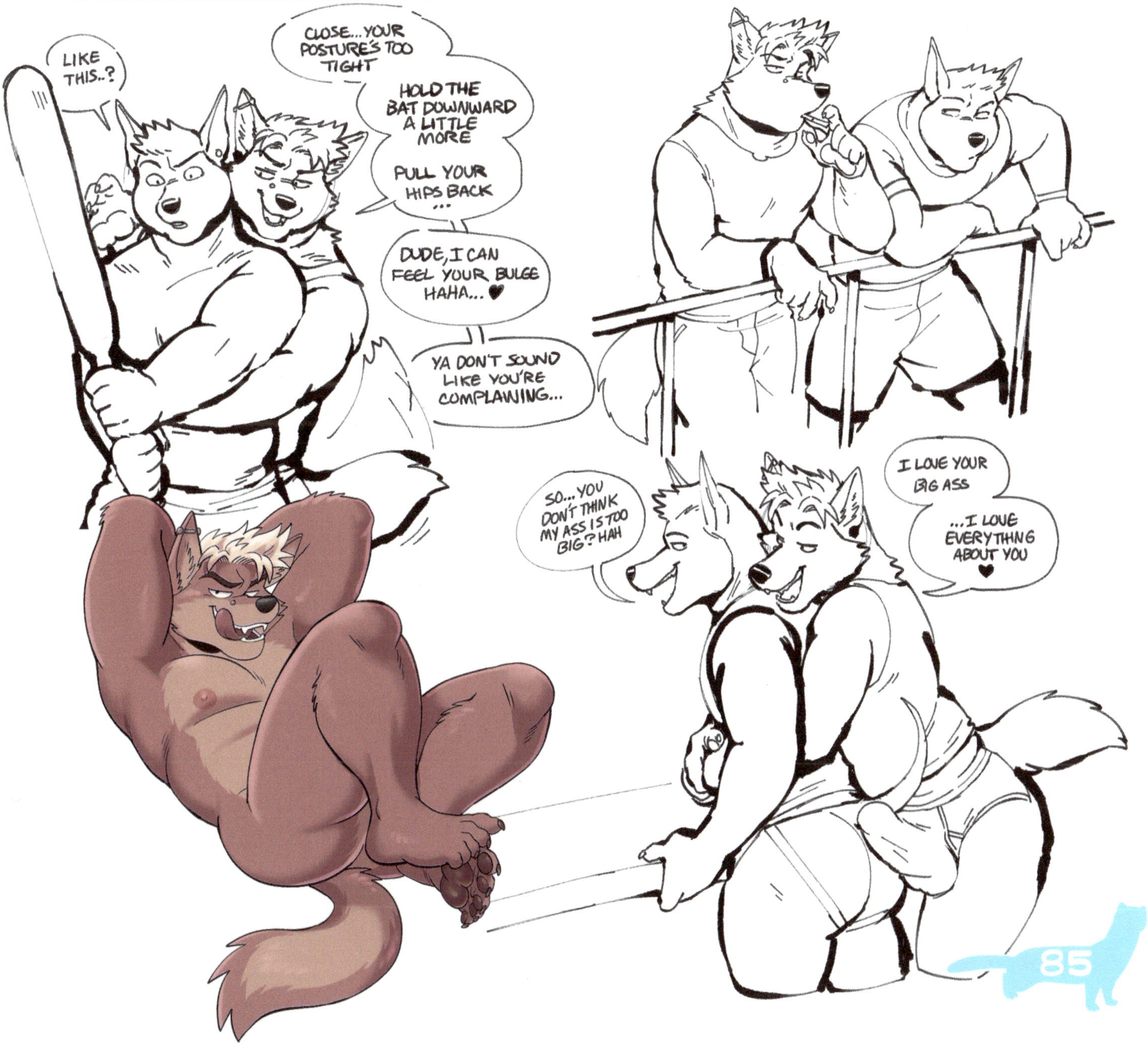

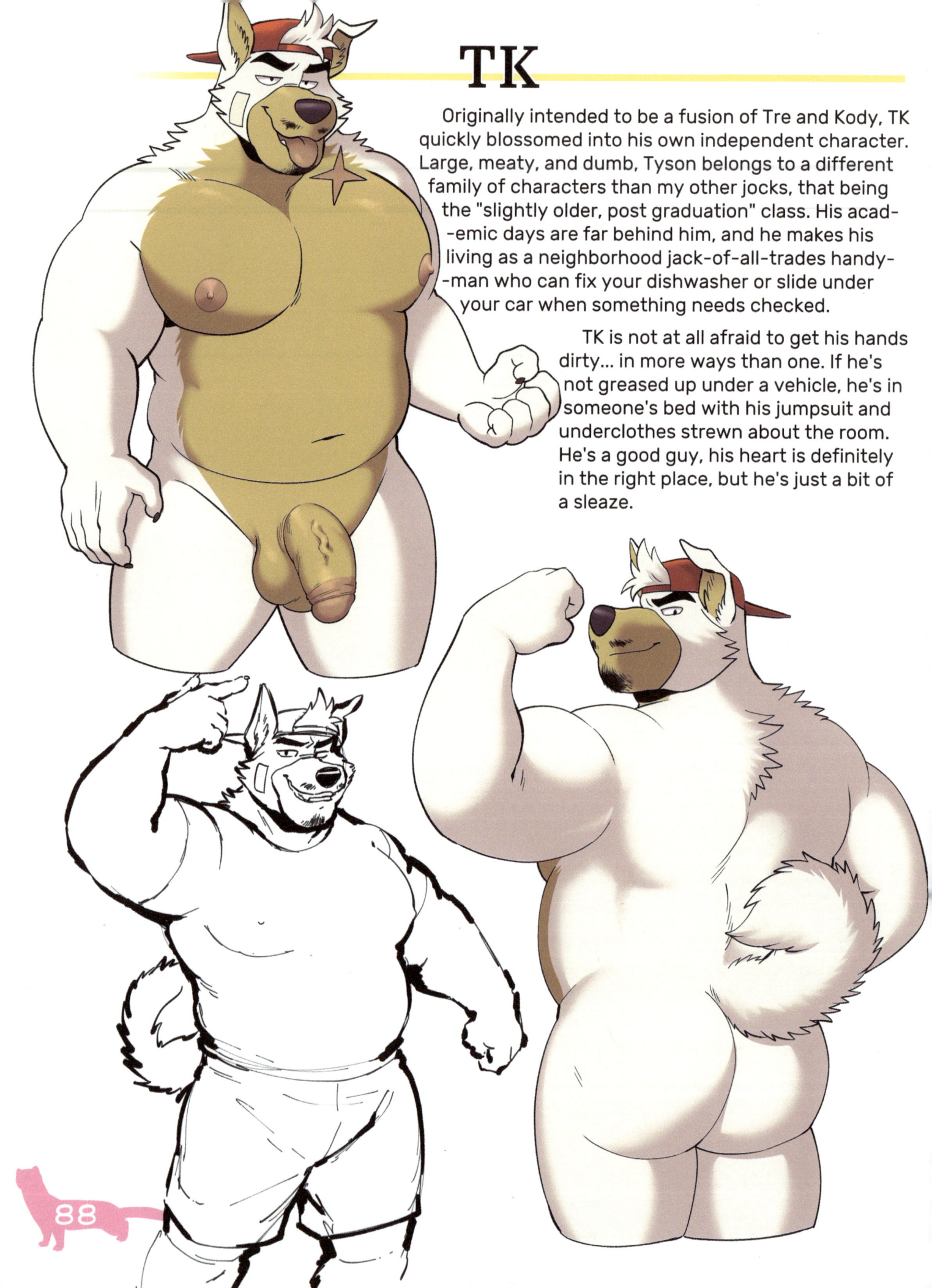

TK

Originally intended to be a fusion of Tre and Kody, TK quickly blossomed into his own independent character. Large, meaty, and dumb, Tyson belongs to a different family of characters than my other jocks, that being the "slightly older, post graduation" class. His acad--emic days are far behind him, and he makes his living as a neighborhood jack-of-all-trades handy--man who can fix your dishwasher or slide under your car when something needs checked.

TK is not at all afraid to get his hands dirty... in more ways than one. If he's not greased up under a vehicle, he's in someone's bed with his jumpsuit and underclothes strewn about the room. He's a good guy, his heart is definitely in the right place, but he's just a bit of a sleaze.

93

Petrol

Born and raised in a rural mountain town, this stoat is accustomed to the small town life - but is very open minded and wants nothing more than to have a good time. Petrol is the definition of a pretty boy twunk who is intelligent but has a warped idea of what is normal for a straight dude. He is skilled with auto mechanics but also makes most of his living online as a gay-for-pay porn star, with the help of his roommate Treble.

An outspoken LGBT ally, Petrol is sincerely in supp--ort of gay rights, same sex marriage, etc. and won't hesitate to say so or defend these things, which is wonderful... but getting drilled by your dire wolf roomie does bring his own sexuality into question. It may be for the sake of his videos, but it is evident he enjoys it a bit more than a straight guy would. Thankfully, he is totally unoffended if teased or questioned about it. In reality, it's more than likely there is some bisexuality under the surface, and he is just aloof to it.

Travis

Troy

103

Coach Marshall Atrata

Humans

Brody

Buck

107

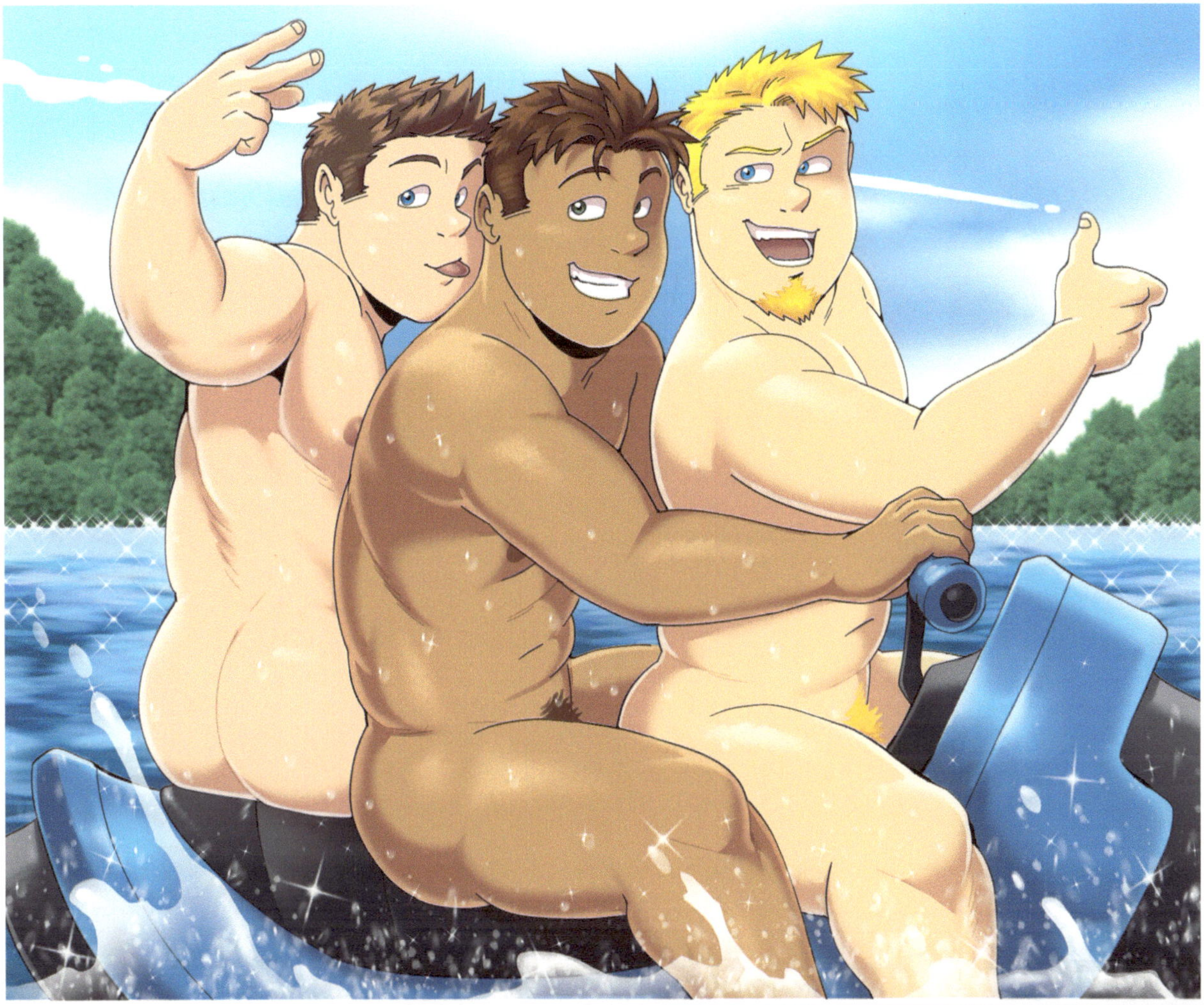

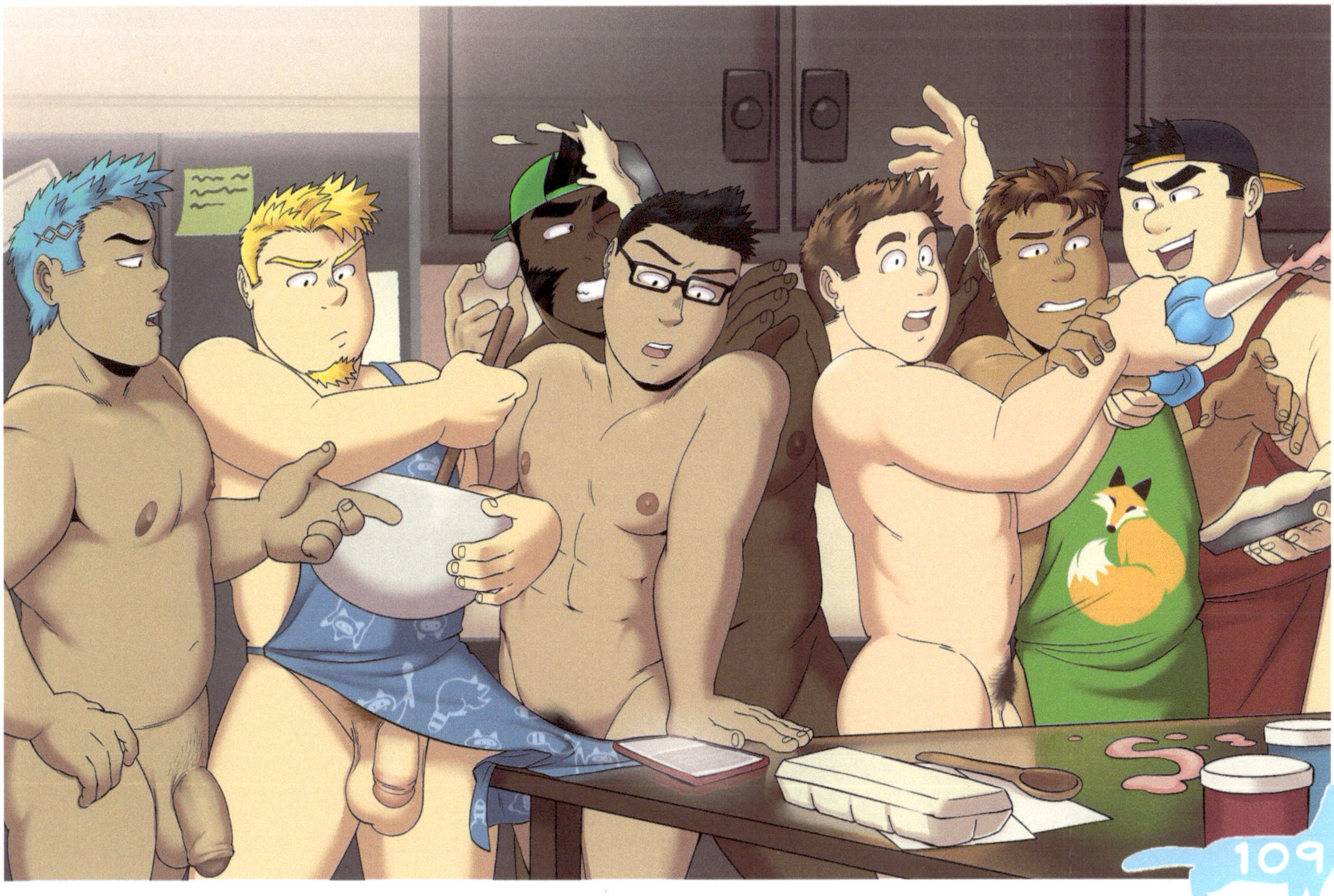

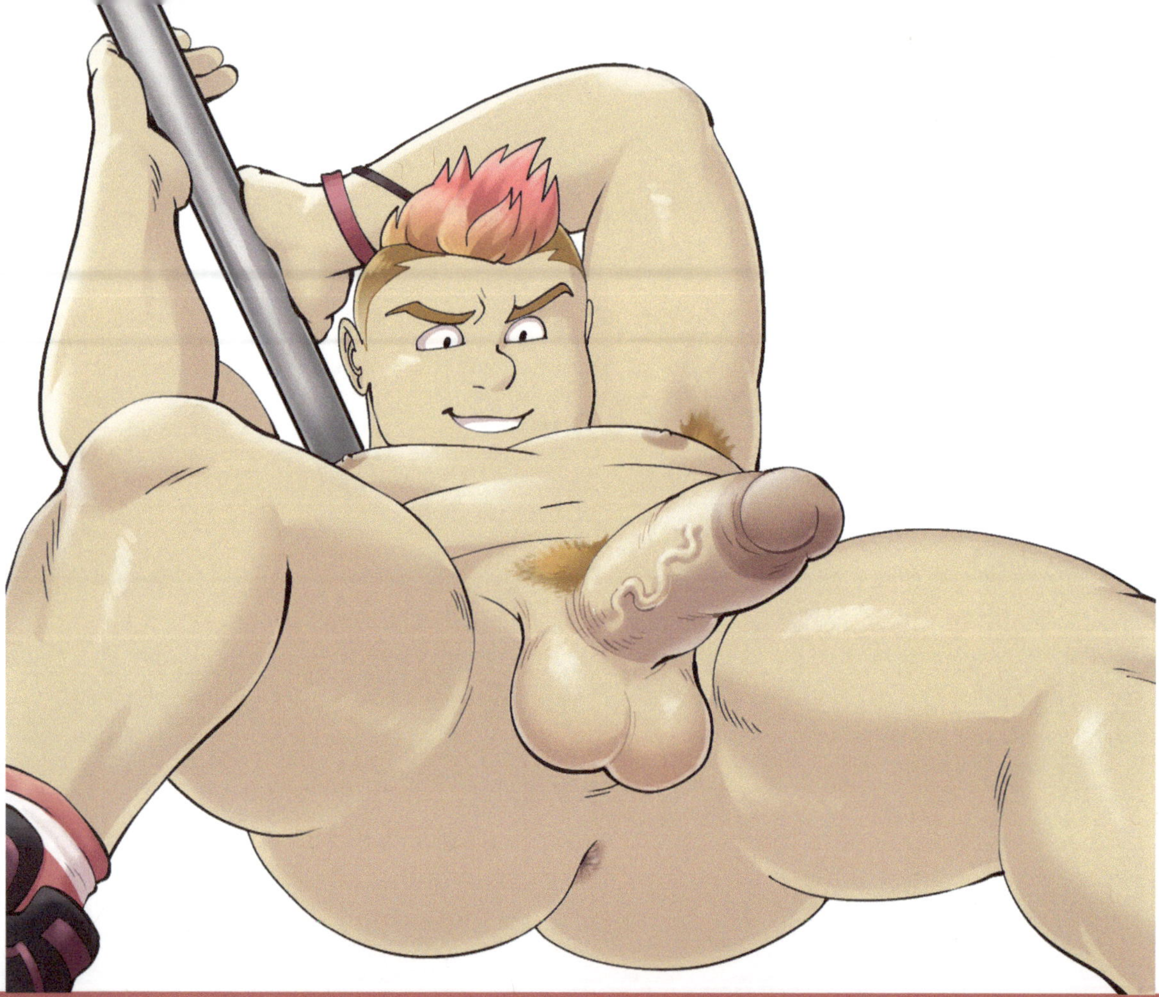

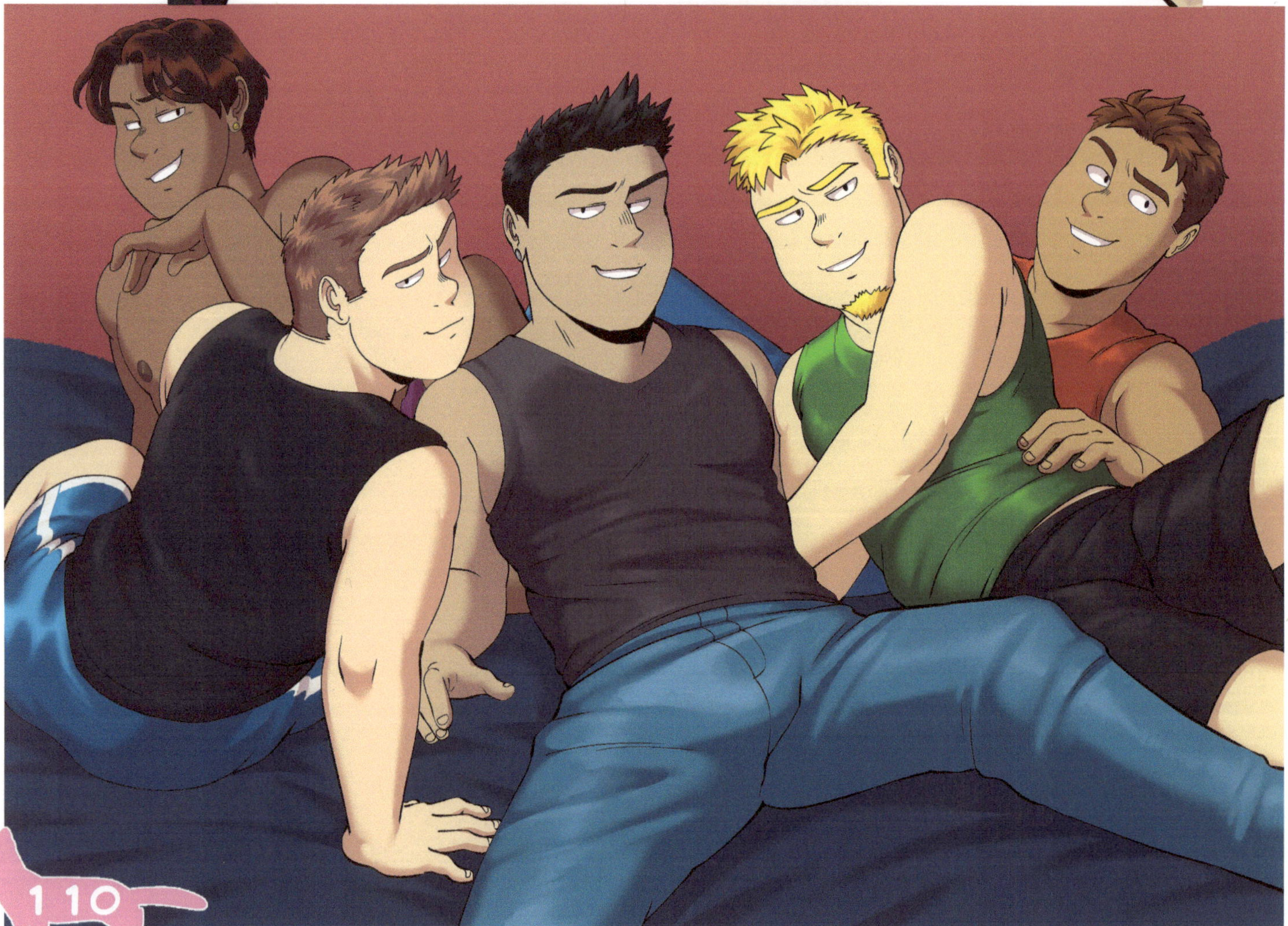